DANGEROUS GAMES

ASTEROID ATTACK

Sue Graves

RISING STARS

Rising Stars UK Ltd.
22 Grafton Street, London W1S 4EX
www.risingstars-uk.com

nasen

NASEN House, 4/5 Amber Business Village, Amber Close,
Amington, Tamworth, Staffordshire B77 4RP

Published 2009

Cover design: pentacor**big**
Illustrations: Rob Lenihan, So Creative Ltd and Paul Loudon
Text design and typesetting: pentacor**big**
Publisher: Gill Budgell
Editorial project management: Lucy Poddington
Editorial consultant: Lorraine Petersen

British Library Cataloguing in Publication Data.
A CIP record for this book is available from the British Library.

ISBN: 978-1-84680-494-6

Printed by Craft Print International Limited, Singapore

CHAPTER 1

Sima, Tom and Kojo were having a day off work. They were going to visit a new observatory called Sky Spy Station, where scientists find out about space.

Sima, Tom and Kojo were good mates. They all worked together at Dangerous Games, a computer games company. Sima designed the games, Kojo programmed them and Tom tested them. The three of them liked to hang out together after work, too.

Professor Giles showed them round the observatory. He took them to see a huge telescope.

"We see into space with this," he said.

"What sort of stuff do you look for?" asked Tom.

"Well, I'm tracking dangers from space, such as asteroids," said the professor. "I'm looking out for any asteroids that might hit Earth."

"What would happen if one did?" asked Kojo.

"It could destroy life on Earth, if it was large enough," said the professor.

"Is that likely to happen?" said Sima nervously.

"Don't worry," laughed the professor. "An asteroid that size only hits Earth about once every 50 million years or so!"

Kojo stared upwards and sighed.

"I wish I could travel through space," he said.
"It would be unreal!"

"I think I can help you there," said the professor.

Kojo, Sima and Tom looked puzzled.

Professor Giles laughed. "Come with me," he said.
"I'll show you what I mean."

The professor led them to a theatre. A film about space was showing on a big screen. He handed Sima, Tom and Kojo some special glasses.

"Put on these 3D glasses. Then sit back and enjoy the film," he said.

Sima, Tom and Kojo put on the glasses.

"This is awesome!" said Tom. "I feel as if I'm really flying through space."

"Amazing!" said Kojo. "Look, we're passing through a meteor shower."

"It's making me feel sick!" wailed Sima, as a comet came rushing towards her. "Get me out of here!"

POP
CORN

After the film they all went for a drink.

Tom looked at his watch and grinned. "We've been out of that theatre for all of five minutes, Sima. I thought you'd have said something by now," he said.

"Something about what?" asked Sima.

Tom laughed. "I thought you'd say, 'Ooh, that film's given me an idea for a new computer game,'" he said, mimicking Sima's voice. "You always say stuff like that."

"I feel too sick to say anything," groaned Sima.
She rubbed her stomach gently.

"But don't you think it would make a great game?" said Kojo.

"What, travelling through space?" said Sima.

"Yeah!" said Tom. "Think about it. In the game you could zoom through space, but you'd have to avoid being hit by comets and asteroids."

"Hmm!" said Sima. She looked thoughtful. "That could work. I'll draw up some ideas at the office tomorrow."

CHAPTER 2

The next day, Sima set to work. She went on the Internet to find out more about space.

Later, she showed her designs to Tom and Kojo.

"I've designed the game so that you start in outer space," she said. "You have to get back to Earth without being hit by asteroids. Each player has an asteroid blaster to explode any asteroids that appear. You get points for every asteroid you blast. It's going to be really cool!"

"So long as the asteroids don't hit Earth," said Kojo. "We don't want to wipe out all human life!"

"Doh!" said Sima, rolling her eyes. "The asteroids are only small. And they won't be heading towards Earth either."

Then Tom had an idea.

"I think this game looks brilliant," he said. "Why don't we test it for real like we've done before?"

"OK then," said Sima. "I'm up for it."

"Don't forget to take some travel pills first," laughed Kojo. "Remember how sick you felt when you wore those 3D glasses!"

"Ugh, don't remind me!" said Sima.

Over the next few days Kojo programmed the game using Sima's designs.

Then he called the other two over. "We'll test the game as usual, after work," he said. "We'll do it when everyone else has gone home."

At six o'clock the office was empty and Sima, Tom and Kojo were ready to test the game.

"Don't we need spacesuits or something?" asked Tom.

"That's all been taken care of in the design," said Sima. "You'll see."

"Remember," said Kojo, "we must all touch the screen at the same time to enter the game. It's only over when we hear the words 'Game over'. OK?"

"OK," said Tom and Sima.

They all touched the screen together. A bright light flashed, hurting their eyes. They shut them tight.

CHAPTER 3

When the light faded, Tom, Sima and Kojo opened their eyes. They were all floating in space.

Tom looked down at the spacesuit he was wearing.

"Neat!" he said. He did a huge somersault.

Sima opened a large pocket on the side of her spacesuit and pulled out a strange-looking weapon. It looked like a long, thin gun. It had sights on the top of the barrel.

"What's that?" asked Tom.

"You've got one, too," said Sima. "This is the special weapon I was telling you about. It's an asteroid blaster for firing missiles at the asteroids."

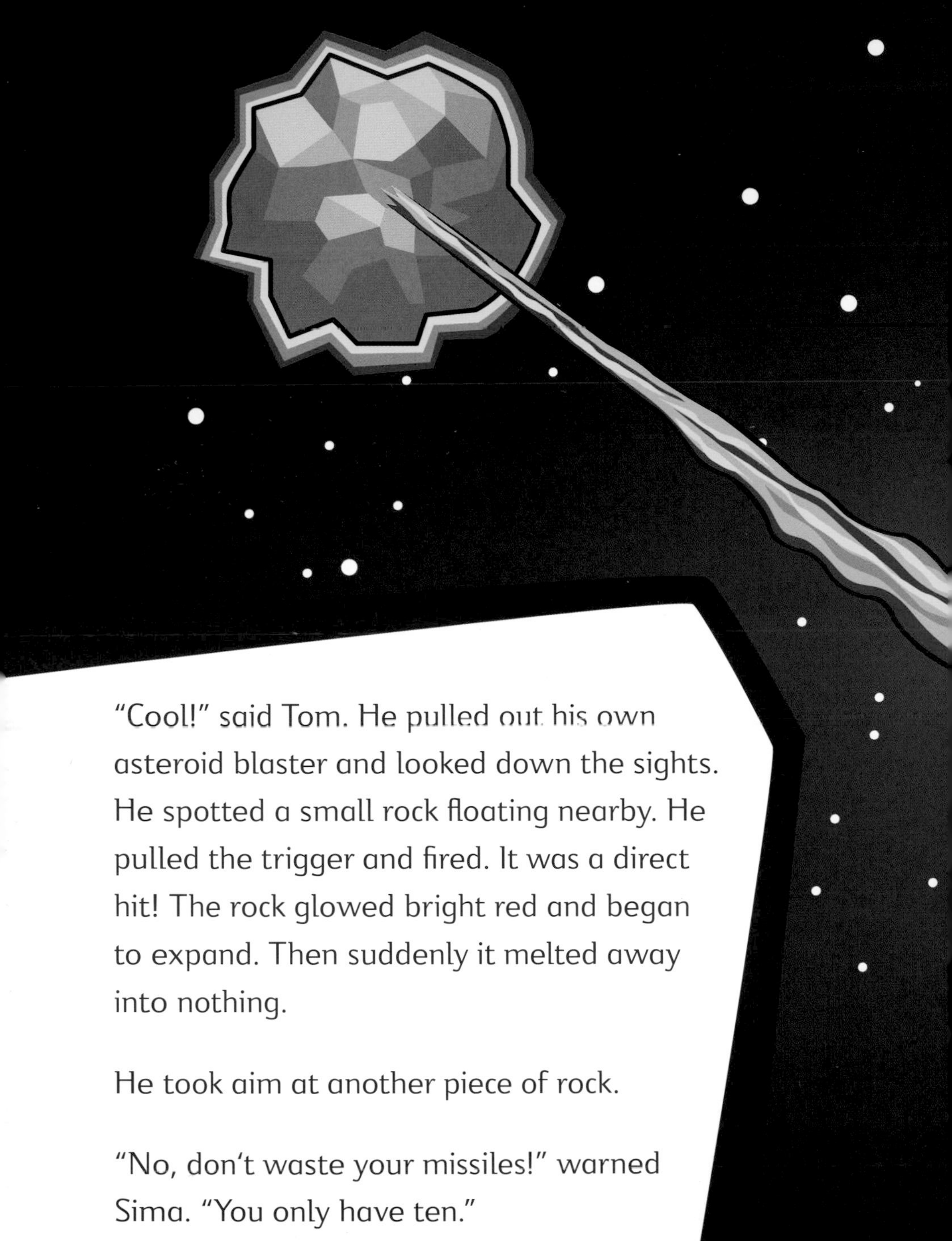

"Cool!" said Tom. He pulled out his own asteroid blaster and looked down the sights. He spotted a small rock floating nearby. He pulled the trigger and fired. It was a direct hit! The rock glowed bright red and began to expand. Then suddenly it melted away into nothing.

He took aim at another piece of rock.

"No, don't waste your missiles!" warned Sima. "You only have ten."

51:00
WOW, SIMA, THIS IS GREAT!

Kojo looked at his watch.

"We're wasting time," he said. "The game will be over before we get back to Earth. If that happens we could end up floating in space for ever."

"But how do we move through space?" asked Tom. "All I can do is float and do somersaults."

Sima pulled at a cord hanging from her shoulder. Flames shot out from a rocket pack on her back. She shot across space.

Tom and Kojo pulled their cords too. All three of them sped towards Earth.

Just then an asteroid came hurtling through space towards them.

"Asteroid attack!" yelled Tom. He aimed his asteroid blaster and fired. It was another direct hit. The asteroid glowed bright red and expanded. Then it melted away.

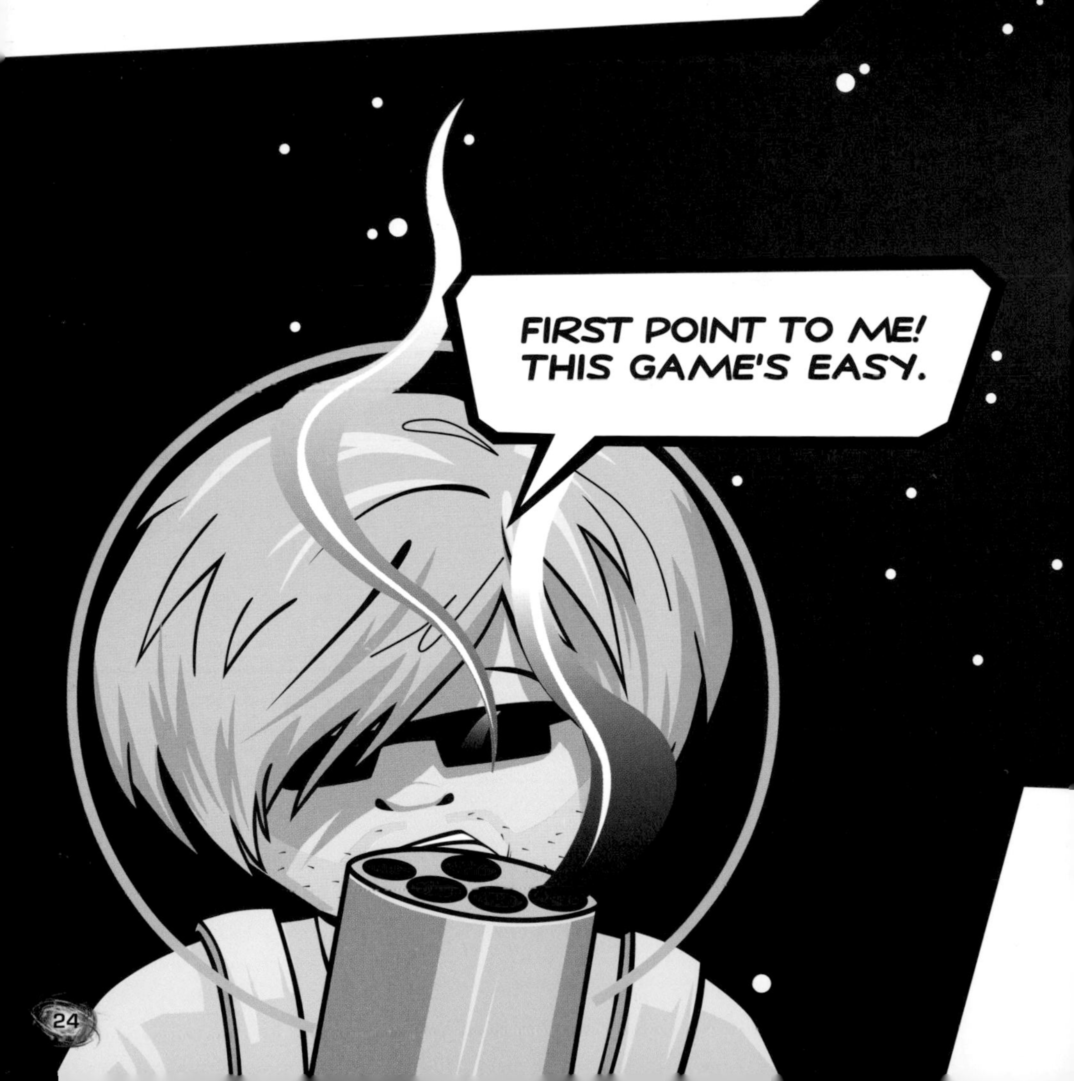

Kojo pointed towards Earth. "Look!" he warned.

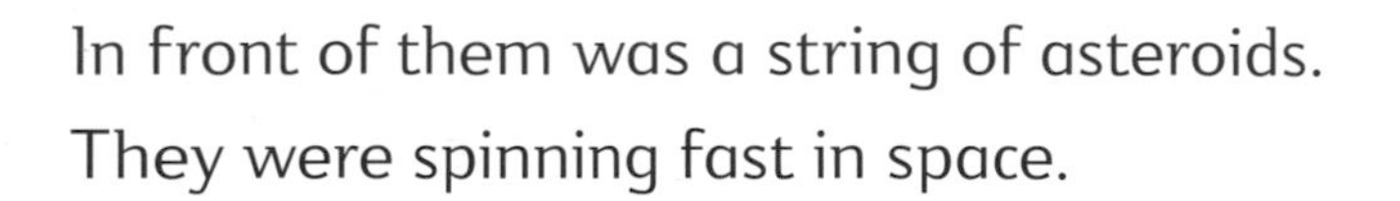

In front of them was a string of asteroids. They were spinning fast in space.

"The asteroids are blocking our path to Earth," said Sima. "We've got to try and blast them out of the way without getting hit ourselves."

They moved nearer to the asteroids. Kojo ducked as one spun close to his head. They aimed their weapons.

30:00
READY, AIM, FIRE!

They fired their weapons again and again until they had hit all the asteroids.

The asteroids glowed bright red and expanded. But this time, they didn't melt away. Instead they exploded in a huge ball of fire.

The force of the explosion pushed Sima, Tom and Kojo backwards. It blew Kojo's weapon out of his hands. Kojo watched in dismay as his asteroid blaster floated away into space.

18:00

DON'T WORRY, WE'RE GETTING CLOSE TO EARTH NOW. STAY NEAR TO US. WE'LL GUARD YOU UNTIL WE'RE SAFELY BACK.

CHAPTER 4

Earth loomed larger and larger in front of them as Kojo, Tom and Sima headed back home. Tom glanced back into space one last time.

A huge asteroid was speeding through space. It was heading straight for Earth!

"I didn't design an asteroid that big," said Sima. "What's happening?"

They stared at the asteroid which was closing in on Earth minute by minute.

"I don't think this is part of the game," Kojo said. "I think this is one of those asteroids that Professor Giles told us about. You know, the ones that hit the Earth every 50 million years or so."

"But th – that means ..." Sima stammered.

"I know," said Kojo. "It means we're about to witness the end of the world!"

Sima checked her weapon. “How many missiles have you got left, Tom?” she asked.

Tom checked. “Only one,” he said.

“I've got two,” said Sima.

"Blasting that asteroid might do more harm than good," said Kojo. "The blasts might push the asteroid faster through space. It could hit Earth with more force than it was going to."

Sima was angry. "Do you have a better idea, Kojo?".

"No, not yet," replied Kojo. "There's got to be a way of saving Earth. But I don't think trying to blow up the asteroid is the answer."

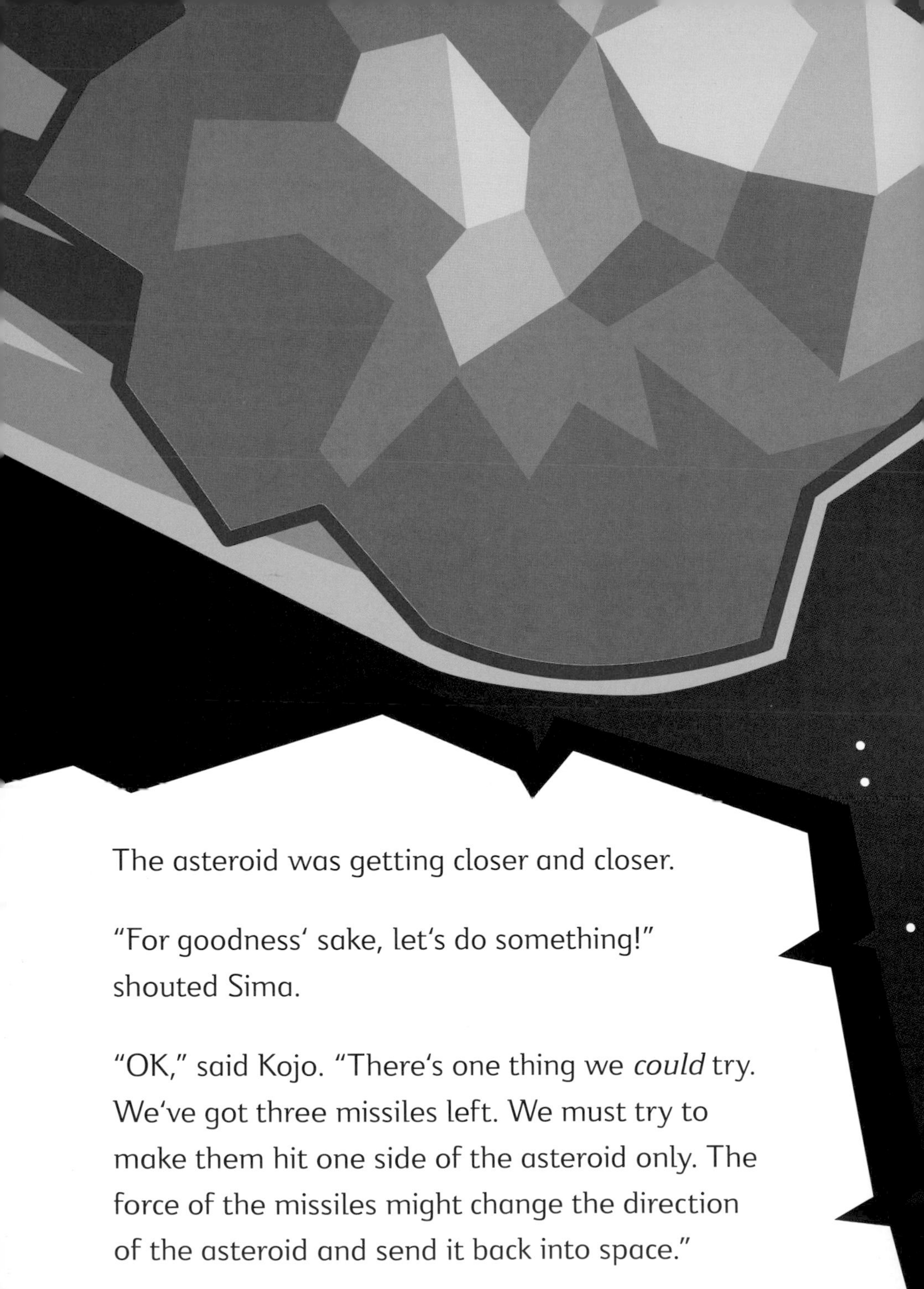

The asteroid was getting closer and closer.

"For goodness' sake, let's do something!" shouted Sima.

"OK," said Kojo. "There's one thing we *could* try. We've got three missiles left. We must try to make them hit one side of the asteroid only. The force of the missiles might change the direction of the asteroid and send it back into space."

05:00
YOU'LL HAVE TO AIM CAREFULLY AT THE LEFT SIDE OF THE ASTEROID.

UNDERSTOOD. LET'S DO IT.

"Wait!" said Kojo. "We've got to let the asteroid get as close to Earth as possible. If we blast it too soon it may have time to get back on track and still hit Earth."

"How long do we have to wait?" asked Tom.

"Looking at the asteroid's speed, I think we should wait two minutes," said Kojo.

Tom looked at his watch. "But there's only two and a half minutes left of the game."

03:00
WE'RE RUNNING OUT OF OPTIONS. WE'VE GOT TO TRY!

CHAPTER 5

The asteroid sped towards them. It was at least a kilometre across. Kojo checked his watch. He gave a signal.

Tom fired his missile. It hit the left side of the asteroid. Pieces of rock split away from it and exploded in balls of hot, red gas. Tom, Sima and Kojo could feel the heat burning through their spacesuits.

Sima fired her first missile. But it missed its target and shot off into space.

"Try again, Sima," yelled Tom. "Hurry up, before it's too late."

Sima aimed carefully. She squeezed the trigger. The missile crashed into the side of the asteroid. Blasts of hot gas shot out from it. The asteroid jerked upwards and then fell away, spinning out into space.

Suddenly they heard a loud voice: "Game over!" The familiar bright light flashed. They shut their eyes.

The next moment, they were back in the office.

Just then Chris Wilson, their boss, came into the room. He had been working late in his office upstairs. He stared at them in their spacesuits.

"What's going on here?" he asked.

"We've been working on a new game," said Sima.

"Excuse me?" said Chris. He looked bewildered.

Tom jabbed Sima in the ribs with his elbow.

"What Sima means is that we did a little extra work on a new game," said Tom. He winked at Sima and Kojo. "But now we're off to a fancy dress party. Aren't we, guys?"

"Yeah, that's it," said Kojo. "A space-themed fancy dress party!" He glanced at the clock. "Hey, look at the time. We'll be late if we don't leave now."

Chris Wilson shook his head and shrugged. "You guys are always dashing about," he said. "You should take things more easily. Anyone would think the world was about to end, the way you rush around."

"I think the world will be OK for another few million years," said Tom.

Sima, Tom and Kojo looked at each other and laughed.

Glossary of terms

3D glasses special glasses which make a film seem real by showing the width, height and depth of things

comet a bright object in space which has a tail of gas and dust

expand to get bigger

meteor shower a shower of shooting stars

missile an object that is shot or thrown as a weapon

observatory a building where people study objects in space using telescopes

program to write a computer game or other computer program

sights a part of a gun that you look through when you take aim

telescope an instrument that makes things far away seem nearer

Quiz

1. Where were Tom, Sima and Kojo going on their day off?
2. What was the name of the professor?
3. What was the professor looking for in space?
4. What was the name of the weapon Sima designed?
5. What colour did things turn when they were hit by a missile?
6. How many missiles did each player have in the game?
7. Who won the first point in the game?
8. Who had two missiles left to aim at the giant asteroid?
9. How long did Kojo say they had to wait before hitting the asteroid?
10. Who was surprised to find Tom, Sima and Kojo in the office after work?

ABOUT THE AUTHOR

Sue Graves has taught for thirty years in Cheshire schools. She has been writing for more than ten years and has written well over a hundred books for children and young adults.

"Nearly everyone loves computer games. They are popular with all age groups – especially young adults. But I've often thought it would be amazing to play a computer game for real. To be in on the action would be the best experience ever! That's why I wrote these stories. I hope you enjoy reading them as much as I've enjoyed writing them for you."

ANSWERS TO QUIZ

1. An observatory called Sky Spy Station
2. Professor Giles
3. Asteroids
4. Asteroid blaster
5. Bright red
6. Ten
7. Tom
8. Sima
9. Two minutes
10. Chris Wilson, their boss